To ....

For being good.

MERRY CHRISTMAS!

From Santa

Santa is coming to the Quad Cities

Written by Steve Smallman
Illustrated by Robert Dunn
Designed by Sarah Allen

Copyright © Hometown World Ltd. 2013

Published by Sourcebooks Jabberwocky, an imprint of Sourcebooks, Inc.
P.O. Box 4410, Naperville, Illinois 60567-4410
(630) 961-3900
Fax: (630) 961-2168
www.jabberwockykids.com

Library of Congress Cataloging-in-Publication data is on file with the publisher.

Source of Production: Worzalla, Stevens Point, WI, USA
Date of Production: September 2013
Run Number: 21289
Printed and bound in USA.
WOZ 10 9 8 7 6 5 4 3 2

Santa is coming to the Quad Cities

Written by Steve Smallman
Illustrated by Robert Dunn

sourcebooks
jabberwocky

"Well?"

boomed Santa. "Have all the children from **the Quad Cities** been good this year?"

"Well...uh...mostly," answered the little old elf, as he bustled across the busy workshop to Santa's desk.

Santa peered down at the elf from behind the tall, teetering piles of letters that the children of the Quad Cities had sent him.

"Mostly?" asked Santa, looking over the top of his glasses.

"Yes...but they've all been **especially** good in the last few days!" said the elf.

"Jolly good!" chuckled Santa,
"Then we'd better get their presents loaded up!"

Even though the sack of presents was

really, really big

and the elves were **really, really** small,

they seemed to have no trouble loading it onto Santa's sleigh.
Though how they managed to fit such a big sack into one little sleigh
even they didn't know. But somehow they did.

"Splendid!" boomed Santa. "We're ready to go!"

"Er...not quite, Santa," said
the little old elf. "One of our
reindeer is missing!"

"Missing?

Which reindeer is missing?" asked Santa.

"The youngest one, Santa," said the elf. "It's his first flight tonight. I've called him and called him, but..."

Just then, a young reindeer strolled up, munching on a large carrot.

"Where have you been?"

asked Santa.

But the youngest reindeer was crunching so loudly that it was no wonder he hadn't heard the little old elf calling.

"Oh well, never mind," said Santa, giving the reindeer a little wink. He took out his Santa-nav and tapped in the coordinates for Iowa and Illinois.
"This will guide us to the Quad Cities in no time."

Crunch!
Crunch!
Crunch!

With a flick of the reins and a jerk of the harness, off they went, racing through the sky.

"Ho, ho, ho!"
laughed Santa.

"We'll soon have all these presents delivered to the girls and boys of the Quad Cities!"

Santa's sleigh flew through the starry night, heading south across the Arctic Ocean. On they flew in the wintry air, high above Canada. In the wink of an eye, the sleigh was flying over Winnipeg and on across Minneapolis.

The youngest reindeer was very excited. He had never been away from the North Pole before.

They had just crossed the Mississippi River
when, suddenly, they ran into a blizzard.
Snowflakes whirled around the sleigh.

They couldn't see a thing!

The youngest reindeer was getting a bit worried,
but Santa didn't seem concerned.

"In two miles..."

said the Santa-nav in a bossy lady's voice,

"...keep left at the next star."

"But, ma'am," Santa blustered, "I can't see any stars in all this snow!"
Soon they were

hopelessly lost!

Ding-dong!
Ding-dong!

Then, through the howling blizzard, the youngest reindeer heard a faint, ringing sound.

Ding-dong!

He looked over at the old reindeer with the red nose. But he had his head down.

(Red nose...I wonder who that could be?!)

Ding-dong!
Ding-dong!

Ding-dong! Ding-dong!

There was that sound again, like church bells ringing. The youngest reindeer turned around to look at Santa. But Santa wasn't listening. He seemed to be arguing with a little box with buttons on it.

With a flick of the harness and a jerk of the reins, the youngest reindeer gave a sharp *tug* and headed off toward the sound of the bells, pulling Santa and his sleigh behind him!

"Whoa!"

cried Santa, pulling his hat straight. "What's going on?" Then, to his surprise, he heard the ringing sound.

"Well done, young reindeer!" he shouted cheerfully, "It must be the bells of Sacred Heart Cathedral in Davenport. Don't worry, children, Santa is coming!"

Then, suddenly...

CRUNCH!

The sleigh hit something as it plummeted through the snow clouds. **"You have arrived!"** said the Santa-nav unhelpfully.

Finally, when the snow had died down and the clouds parted, Santa discovered exactly where they were...

...stuck, right at the very top of a **Christmas tree** near the **Antoine Leclaire House!**

"Everybody, PULL!"

The reindeer *pulled* with all their might until, at last, with a screeching noise, the sleigh scraped clear of the Christmas tree. Santa steered them safely above the Davenport Library, past Centennial Bridge, over Broadway Historic District, and down into Longview Park.

Luckily, there
was no real
damage done, but
the packages had all
been jumbled up. Santa
quickly sorted out the
presents into order again.

"All right," said Santa. "Thanks
to this young reindeer I know where
we are now. Don't worry, children,

Santa is coming!"

Santa drove his sleigh expertly
from rooftop to rooftop all over the
Quad Cities, popping in and out of
chimneys as fast as he could go.

(Which was
pretty fast
for a chubby
fellow!)

There were big chimneys in Moline and small
chimneys in Bettendorf. He squeezed down thin
chimneys in Davenport and plummeted
down fat chimneys in Rock Island.

The youngest reindeer was
amazed at how quickly they went.
Santa never seemed to get tired at all!
And it looked like all the children in
the Quad Cities were going to be very
lucky this year! But the youngest
reindeer was starting to feel
a bit weary and quite
hungry too!

He piled them under the Christmas trees
and carefully filled up the stockings
with surprises.

In house after house, Santa delved
inside his sack for packages of
every shape and size.

Santa took a little bite out of each cookie, a tiny sip of milk, wiped his beard, and popped the carrots into his sack.

In house after house, the good children of the Quad Cities had left out a plate of cookies, a small glass of milk, and a big, crunchy carrot.

From Buffalo to Kewanee, from Bluegrass to Silvis, from East Moline to Old Town Chicago, and ALL the places in between, Santa and his sleigh visited every house in the Quad Cities.

Santa delivered presents to Ava, Aiden,
Benjamin, Brooklyn, Carter, Chloe...
the list went on and on! ...Yazmine,
Zachary, Zander, Zybil.

(Zybil? That
must be a spelling
mistake, surely!)

SUPERMARKET

Finally, Santa had delivered the last present on his long Quad Cities list.

"Great moons and stars!" sighed Santa. "It's past midnight and my sack seems as heavy as ever! I hope I haven't forgotten anyone."

Santa opened his sack to check...but it was full of juicy, crunchy carrots!

Santa divided the carrots among all the reindeer.
"Well, done!" he said, patting the youngest reindeer gently on the nose.

But the youngest reindeer didn't hear him...he was too busy munching!

Then it was time to set off for home. Santa reset his Santa-nav once more to the North Pole, and soon they were speeding above Niabi Zoo and high over Eagle Point Park through the crisp, starry night.